PIPPBROOK BOOKS

First published in the UK in 1999 by Templar Publishing
This softback edition produced in the UK in 2015 by Pippbrook Books,
an imprint of Templar Publishing,
part of the Bonnier Publishing Group,
The Plaza, 535 King's Road, London, SW10 0SZ
www.templarco.co.uk
www.bonnierpublishing.com

ISBN 978-1-84877-881-8

Designed by Hayley Bebb and Manhar Chauhan
Edited by Dugald Steer and Liza Miller

Printed in Malaysia

PIPPBROOK
P
BOOKS

The Little LOST DUCKLING

WRITTEN BY SUE BARRACLOUGH   ILLUSTRATIONS BY SIMON MENDEZ

One sunny morning, Mother Duck led her
four new ducklings down to the old pond.
"Stay close, little ones," she told them.

But one little duckling didn't listen.

"Follow me, my babies," called Mother Duck as she swam away.
But one little duckling didn't do as she was told.
She didn't want to follow her mother across the water.

She wanted to dart after the dragonflies,

watch the frogs hopping
on the lily pads

and chase the glistening fish.

So that's just what Little Duckling did.

She splashed in the water and frightened the fish. She snapped her little beak at the dragonflies. She quacked in amazement when the beautiful kingfisher flew by.

After a while, Little Duckling was tired of playing.
She scrambled up onto the grassy bank and
fluffed out her feathers to dry.
Around her the wind whispered in the grass.
The leaves rustled, and overhead the sky grew dark.

Little Duckling realised she was all alone.

Little Duckling looked out across the pond.
Mother Duck was nowhere to be seen.
Suddenly, Little Duckling wanted to see
her mother very much indeed.
Just then, Hedgehog came shuffling by.

"Have you seen my mummy?" asked Little Duckling.
But Hedgehog just shook his head, and carried
on hunting for juicy worms to eat.

So Little Duckling walked a little further
down the bank until she met Squirrel.
"Have you seen my mummy?" she asked again.

But Squirrel was too busy collecting acorns
to even answer, so Little Duckling had to
carry on walking.

She hadn't gone very far before she met Rabbit.
"Who are you?" the rabbit asked.
"I'm a lost duckling and I'm looking for my mummy."
"Then you should stay by the water, or Mr Fox will get you,"
said Rabbit. And with a flash of his white tail
he disappeared beneath the ground.

Little Duckling wasn't feeling very brave at all now.
She quacked loudly, hoping her mummy might hear.
"I wouldn't do that if I were you," said a squeaky voice.
"Mr Fox might hear you!" It was Mouse.
"Oh dear, oh dear!" cheeped Little Duckling.
"Please help me find Mother Duck."
But the mouse had scurried away.

Just then, a big, furry beaver scrambled onto the bank.
"Hrrumph!" he grunted. "What's a little duckling
like you doing here, all on your own?"

"I'm lost and I'm looking for my mummy!"
wailed the poor little duckling.

"Is she a nice, brown, cuddly mummy?" asked Beaver.
"Who told you always to stay close by her side?"

Little Duckling nodded sadly.
"Then you'll find her looking for YOU
over by those reeds," said Beaver.

"Mummy!" quacked the little duckling happily.
"I promise to never wander off again."

And do you know what? She never, ever did.